To
Bella, Lia and Alexa.
xxx

Published in the United Kingdom by:

Blue Falcon Publishing
The Mill, Pury Hill Business Park,
Alderton Road, Towcester
Northamptonshire, NN12 7LS
Email: books@bluefalconpublishing.co.uk
Web: www.bluefalconpublishing.co.uk

A CIP record of this book is available from the British Library.

First printed 2018
ISBN 978-1912765089

Pete The Cheeky Parakeet

Cheryl Lee-White

We once had a little bright green parakeet,
he wasn't a very nice fellow to meet.

He would squeak and squawk and peck at our hair,
swooping at us as he flew through the air.
Although he was a pretty and clever little bird,
his attitude, sadly, was so absurd.

He was called Pete our pet parakeet.
He had a beautiful shiny red-coloured beak
with vibrant green feathers that feel silky smooth,
and claw-like feet to help him when on the move.

Pete was unkind to everyone –
everyone, that is except my mum.
Everywhere she went he would follow,
without her he was full of sorrow.

If our dog Max went near my mum,
Pete would peck him in the bum!

If we hugged mum while Pete was there,
he would try to poop in our hair.

One day my mum came home with some news.
Her work was sending her away on a cruise!
She would be sailing across the sea,
she tried to hide it but she was so happy.

As it was work only she would be going away,
with my dad the rest of us would stay.
Although we felt a bit sad we didn't mind —
that's because our Dad is very funny and kind.

I think Pete will suffer when Mum has left,
and start to feel a bit depressed.
This is because without my mum,
I am sad to say he will have no one.

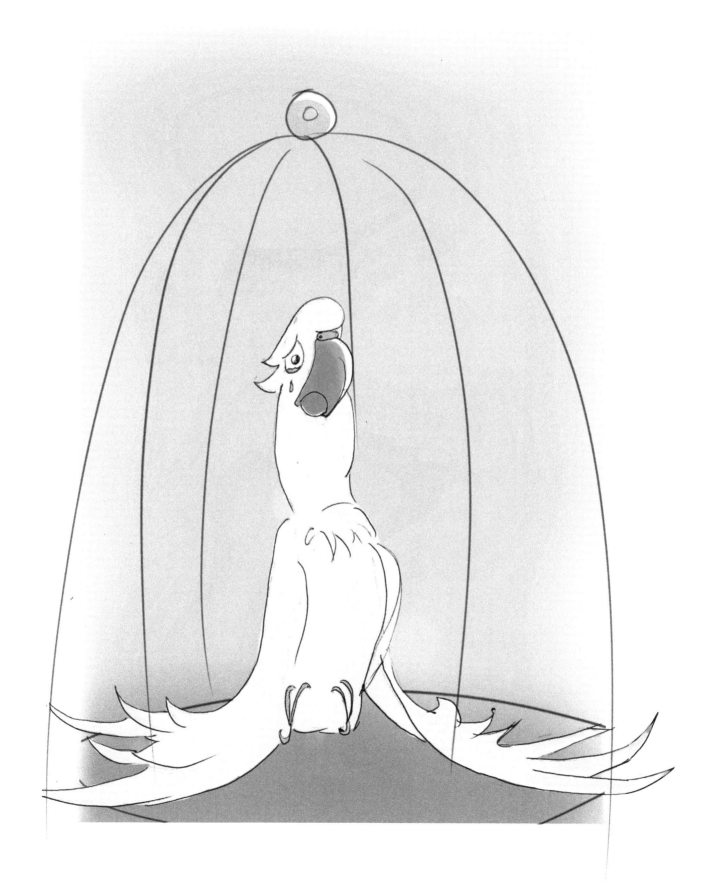

The day came for my mum to depart.
We felt a little bit sad in our hearts,
but we knew she would be coming back soon —
she would only be gone for one week of June.

When Pete realised Mum hadn't come home,
He looked sad and started to feel all alone.

He perched there all night looking glum in his cage,
we dare not go near him in case he got in a rage.
My mum was the only friend in our house he had,
that's because his behaviour to the rest of us was so bad.

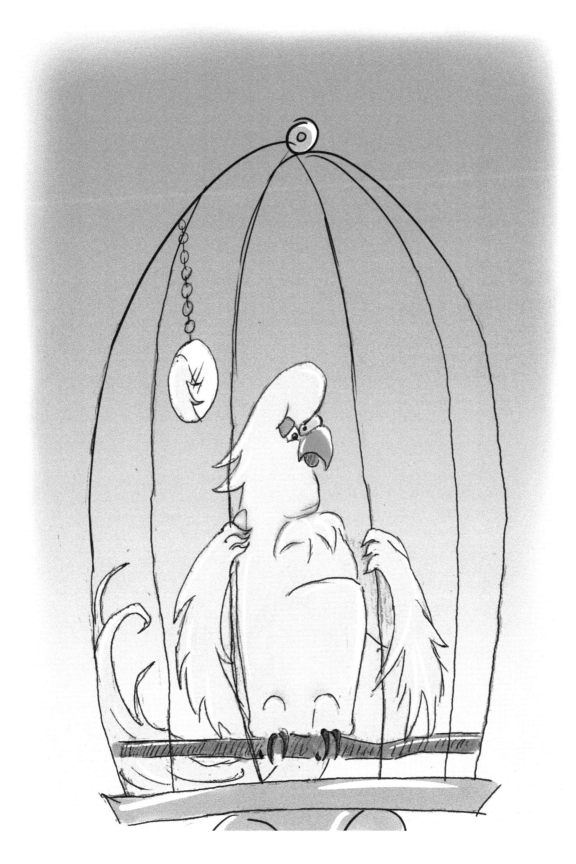

Day after day, Pete would be looking very lonely and sad,
while the rest of us all enjoyed lots of laughs with our dad.

One day, we were playing and having fun.
We made an obstacle course for Max to run.

We were smiling and laughing, enjoying the time,
Max's tail wagged with every climb.
I caught sight of Pete across the room,
he looked so sad perched there in the gloom.

We couldn't let Pete be alone anymore.
I slowly put my hand into his cage door.
I was scared he would peck at my finger –
I thought he would act like a real stinker.

He edged towards me looking all shameful,
he knew his behaviour had been so disgraceful.
Although he had been mean, that could be forgotten,
that is only as long as he stops being rotten.

"Pete," I announced, "you are welcome to play."
"As long as he's nice," I heard my brother say.
Pete flew out and gracefully landed on my arm
and then he began to turn on the charm.

"I am sorry," cried Pete "for being so mean.
All the things that I have done were so obscene
I have learnt my lesson; I'll be nice to everyone."
Then he asked "I would really love to join in your fun."

Pete joined in and we had fun together.
Everyone especially Pete felt much better.
Not only did Pete still have love from my mum;
He was now well-behaved and friends with everyone.

Being friendly to everybody is always the best way,
it will make everyone happy and brighten up the day.

SPOT THE DIFFERENCE

Can you SPOT the differences between the two pictures? There are seven to find.

Blue Falcon
Publishing

Blue Falcon Publishing is an independent UK publisher, specialising in full-colour picture books.
Our aim is to bring creative stories to engage young children in reading from an early age.
www.bluefalconpublishing.co.uk
email: books@bluefalconpublishing.co.uk
facebook: @bluefalconpublishing

ABOUT THE AUTHOR

Raised in Epsom, Surrey, Cheryl now lives in Taunton, Somerset, with her partner and three beautiful girls aged 10, 8, and 7. A love of reading, inspired by travel books and non-fiction biographies, led to a desire to write – more specifically, to write for her children. Cheryl blogs about her life with her girls and often includes self-penned rhymes for her readers, so a rhyming children's book seemed the obvious choice!

You can find out more about Cheryl and read her blog at www.thesimplemum.com.

Lightning Source UK Ltd.
Milton Keynes UK
UKHW05f1543031018
329901UK00005B/67/P